Dear Parents:

Congratulations! Your child is taking the first steps on an exciting journey. The destination? Independent reading!

STEP INTO READING® will help your child get there. The program offers five steps to reading success. Each step includes fun stories and colorful art or photographs. In addition to original fiction and books with favorite characters, there are Step into Reading Non-Fiction Readers, Phonics Readers and Boxed Sets, Sticker Readers, and Comic Readers—a complete literacy program with something to interest every child.

Learning to Read, Step by Step!

Ready to Read   Preschool–Kindergarten
• big type and easy words • rhyme and rhythm • picture clues
For children who know the alphabet and are eager to begin reading.

Reading with Help   Preschool–Grade 1
• basic vocabulary • short sentences • simple stories
For children who recognize familiar words and sound out new words with help.

Reading on Your Own   Grades 1–3
• engaging characters • easy-to-follow plots • popular topics
For children who are ready to read on their own.

Reading Paragraphs   Grades 2–3
• challenging vocabulary • short paragraphs • exciting stories
For newly independent readers who read simple sentences with confidence.

Ready for Chapters   Grades 2–4
• chapters • longer paragraphs • full-color art
For children who want to take the plunge into chapter books but still like colorful pictures.

STEP INTO READING® is designed to give every child a successful reading experience. The grade levels are only guides; children will progress through the steps at their own speed, developing confidence in their reading. The F&P Text Level on the back cover serves as another tool to help you choose the right book for your child.

Remember, a lifetime love of reading starts with a single step!

All rights reserved. Published in the United States by Random House Children's Books, a division of Random House LLC, a Penguin Random House Company, New York. This work is adapted from *Everything Happens to Aaron in the Autumn* by P. D. Eastman, copyright © 1967 by Random House LLC. The artwork that appears herein originally appeared in *Everything Happens to Aaron in the Autumn* and in *The Cat in the Hat Beginner Book Dictionary. The Cat in the Hat Beginner Book Dictionary* by the Cat himself and P. D. Eastman, copyright © 1964 and renewed 1992 by Random House LLC.

Step into Reading, Random House, and the Random House colophon are registered trademarks of Random House LLC.

Visit us on the Web!
StepIntoReading.com
randomhousekids.com

Educators and librarians, for a variety of teaching tools, visit us at RHTeachersLibrarians.com

Library of Congress Cataloging-in-Publication Data
Eastman, P. D. (Philip D.)
Aaron loves apples and pumpkins / by P. D. Eastman.
pages cm. — (Step into reading. Step 1)
"This work is adapted from Everything Happens to Aaron in the Autumn by P. D. Eastman, copyright © 1967 by Random House LLC."
Summary: Aaron the alligator cannot seem to do anything right, whether it be playing hide-and-seek, picking apples, or playing football.
ISBN 978-0-553-51234-2 (trade pbk.) — ISBN 978-0-553-51235-9 (lib. bdg.) — ISBN 978-0-553-51236-6 (ebook)
[1. Ability—Fiction. 2. Autumn—Fiction. 3. Alligators—Fiction. 4. Humorous stories.] I. Title.
PZ7.E1314Aak 2015 [E]—dc23 2014025552

Printed in the United States of America

10 9 8 7 6 5 4 3 2 1

This book has been officially leveled by using the F&P Text Level Gradient™ Leveling System.

STEP INTO READING®

STEP 1
READY TO READ

Aaron
Loves Apples
and Pumpkins

by P. D. Eastman

Random House 🏠 New York

This is Aaron.

Aaron is an alligator.

Aaron and his friends
play hide-and-seek.

Maybe he will hide
behind the barrel.

Maybe he will hide
under the barrel.

They found Aaron
in the barrel!

How did they know
he was in there?

Aaron and his friends
watch football.

11

Aaron and his friends
play football.

Aaron can kick.

Aaron can catch.

Aaron can run.

Tackle!

His friends are
good at football, too!

Aaron is ready

for Halloween.

His friends
like his costume.

These kids are afraid
of the ghost.

Oops!
The ghost tripped
and fell.

It is not a ghost.

It is Aaron!

How did she know
it was him?

Aaron's friends
are picking apples.

Aaron knows
a better way.

Aaron shows them.

Thump! Thump! Thump!

Down come the apples.

Aaron sure knew
a better way!